mabel frye
accidental private eye

mabel frye: accidental private eye

A Prequel Novella

kayt miller

about mabel frye

Accidental Private Eye: A Prequel Novella

Meet Mabel Frye. Librarian by day, super sleuth by night.

Wait a second, that's not how Mabel's story begins.

Mabel, a Chicago native, finds herself jobless due to budget cuts and homeless thanks to her cheating ex.

After living with her best friend for a bit, Mabel discovers she's inherited a house in Savannah, Georgia from her beloved grandmother.

With nothing to lose except her pride and possibly her mind, Mabel sets out for a new adventure—a fresh start at a library in the heart of the historic district.

Only things don't go all that well for Mabel. No one at the library will give her a chance no matter how hard she tries and that is discouraging.

Getting framed for murder by one of those same employees, well, that's just beyond the pale.

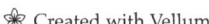

contents

I dedicate this book to my biggest cheerleader. My mom.

chapter one

"THIS IS THE LAST ONE." MISTY JONES, THE *BEST*, BEST FRIEND A GIRL could ask for, says as she plops the cardboard box onto the floor next to my new front door. Well, not new. It's very old, actually. It's new to me, though.

I stare at the stacks of boxes that fill the parlor of this ancient house and frown. "Can you believe you're staring at my entire life right now?"

"No." Misty sidles up to me and throws an arm over my shoulders. "This is the shit that you drag through life; it's *not* your 'life.'" She does air quotes with one hand. She's talented like that. "And while we're on the subject, I'm just going to tell you now, this is the last time I'm schlepping your stupid books for you."

I do have a ton of books. Literally. A *ton*. What can I say? I'm in the book business. Plus, I love to read more than anything in the world, especially real books. Sure, I'll read on my tablet, but it's not the same as the feel of actual pages between my fingers. The books in these boxes are like old friends to me. How could I ever part with them?

"Either donate them to your library or hire some movers." Her eyes grow round. "Ooh, did you see there's a new moving company out there?"

I shake my head.

"Yeah. It's called something like College Hunks Moving Company."

I snicker. "Really?"

She nods excitedly. "I saw a truck on the tollway last week and almost chased it down so I could see who was driving the truck."

"Why? So you could see if they were, in fact, 'Hunks'?" Yeah. I could do one-handed air quotes too.

"Of course," Misty scoffs. "What kind of investigative journalist would I be if I didn't follow up on a lead?"

"A bad one." I nod.

"That's correct. And I am the best in the biz."

"You are indeed the best, my friend." I step out from under Misty's arm and head in the direction of the kitchen. "Let's have a beer and sit on the front porch."

"Great idea."

With the cheapest domestic beer I could get at the convenience store down the road, Misty and I make our way out the front door. I sigh when the fresh air hits my lungs. The temperature is perfect in Georgia this time of year. March is not too hot, not too cold. Not that it ever gets as cold as it gets in Chicago, my hometown. But it sure gets hotter. Summer in Savannah is sweltering.

"I can't believe you're leaving me alone in Chicago." Misty sighs as she sips her beer. "I'm going to miss the crap out of you."

I feel the burn of tears, but I refuse to cry. Yet. "You could move down here." I try to laugh at my words, but I'm not joking. "This old place has three bedrooms. We could be roomies again, just like we were in college." Seems like eons ago when we were in college. That's where we met. At the University of Illinois, Urbana. We were both English majors as undergrads and became fast friends due to our mutual crush on Professor Belker in English Composition. God, that man was h-o-t. I bet he's still gorgeous even ten years later.

"You know I can't leave Chicago."

Sadness hits me right in the heart. "I know."

"It's no coincidence that your grandmother left you this place now."

One thing about Misty you should know, she has more common sense than most people, but she's also a true believer in fate. One of her favorite expressions is "Everything happens for a reason."

I get what she means. My grandmother's death didn't come as a surprise. She was in her late eighties and had a number of health issues. What was a surprise was her will. Of her ten grandchildren, she left this house to me, her namesake. She included a year of taxes and insurance paid along with a small nest egg for repairs in that inheritance too. I adored my grandmother and visited every summer until I was fifteen—after that, silly teenage priorities took its place. I wish someone would have told me I'd regret not spending every possible moment with her.

I glance back at the front of the house and sigh. This place has really deteriorated since the last time I was here. The white paint is peeling from the exterior. Several of the black shutters are hanging by a thread. There's at least one broken window, and the roof looks like it should've been replaced a decade ago. Inside, well, let's just say the nest egg she left me isn't going to scratch the surface. If I had to guess, I'd say the place needs repairs from the inside out and top to bottom. I doubt five thousand dollars is going to cut it. It's a start, though.

The fact is, Misty is right. This all happened at the precise moment I needed it the most. I'd lost my job due to budget cuts, my boyfriend of two and a half years due to his cheating, and the apartment I shared with him due to his name being the only one on the lease. Because of all that, I was sleeping on Misty's couch and had been for two months when I got the news about Grandma Mabel.

"I hope that library of yours has some good DIY books." Misty gestures at the house. "Because it's in bad shape."

"I'm sure they have an excellent Do It Yourself collection." Most libraries do these days.

"You start on Monday?"

I nod. I start a brand-new job at the Chatham County Public Libraries here in Savannah. Once again, fate seems to have stepped in because library jobs are few and far between, but the day I started the job hunt, a position as Library Manager of the Forsyth Street branch opened up. I applied, interviewed a week later over Zoom, and was offered the job a week after that. See? Fate.

I smile at my dearest friend and raise my empty beer can. "To new beginnings?"

She taps her empty against mine. "And to, hopefully, some great adventures."

"I'll drink to that."

chapter two

WHILE I BAWL MY EYES OUT WATCHING MISTY'S PLANE FLY OFF, I realize two things. One, I already hate that my best friend will soon be a thousand miles away, and two, why the hell did I think I could do this? How could I move to Isle of Hope, Georgia, a suburb of Savannah? Alone?

I don't have an answer to that one except to say, I didn't really have any other options. The part-time job as a barista at the little coffee shop near Misty's place wasn't cutting it. I was able to defer my student loans for a little while, but those will be due again soon. Plus, I needed to get away from Curt. My ex. He kept popping up in the strangest places. While I tend to believe it was just a coincidence because the jerk made it crystal clear he was done with me, Misty thought he was stalking me.

I scoffed at that because if there's one thing I know about Curt Young, he's too lazy to stalk anybody. Especially me.

After I can no longer see Misty's plane, I walk slowly back to my Prius. There's no need to rush. I've got nothing pressing to do because in the three days she was here, the two of us unpacked everything but my books and scrubbed my house from top to bottom. We even had time for a tour of Savannah's historic district.

I'm telling you, if you've never been to Savannah, Georgia,

you need to make the trek. It's absolutely beautiful. Not to mention it's full of history—and ghosts. Lots and lots of ghosts. Hell, there's even a ghost walking tour. Grandma Mabel and I took that tour years ago. The stories made sense to me then. I'm not so jaded now that I don't believe in them. Remember the whole fate thing? Well, believing in fate isn't much of a departure from accepting the possibility that dead people are walking around haunting stuff.

Behind the wheel of my beat-up car, I sigh. I'm avoiding the inevitable loneliness that will hit the second I step into my grandmother's house. Tapping my steering wheel, I ponder my options. I could go home and sulk, or I could do something. The night is young. It's not even nine o'clock in the evening yet.

I know where I could go. Pinkie Masters. A cute little dive bar Misty and I found last night on our final adventure. It had the best juke box I've ever seen with classic songs from the seventies and eighties. Even though I'm in my late twenties, I recognize most of the tunes because I grew up listening to them in my parents' car. Those songs ran on repeat thanks to their cassette player. As for this clientele, well, it looks as though many of them had seen better days, but that's okay, they were fun. "Where was that place again?" I pick up my phone and search for the address. Ah, right. "Drayton Street." Shifting into drive, I feel a renewed sense of purpose.

I find a parking spot a block from Pinkie's. Slipping out, I'm about to press the lock on my key fob when I remember how my grandma felt about her city. She never locked her door, saying, "The Isle of Hope was the safest place on earth."

Even though it's been almost fifteen years since my last visit, it doesn't feel like it's changed. Savannah is idyllic and a bit surreal.

Stepping into Pinkie's, I feel a tiny bit nervous. It wasn't that way with Misty by my side because she's the kind of friend that has your back, no matter what. With her, I know I can face anything. But now, I have to go it alone. Luckily, I recognize one of the old fellas from last night. Sliding into the empty seat next to him, I tap his shoulder as he looks in the other direction. "Hey, Barney."

His head jerks my way, catching me off guard. "Who the hell are you?"

Okay. First of all, I saw him *last night*. Second of all…. My thoughts trail off when I realize he must've been drunk. "Um. I'm Mabel."

"Mabel?" He frowns. "You're too young to have an old lady name."

Funny. He said the same thing to me last night. "I'm named after my grandmother."

"Well, that's too bad."

He said that too.

I'm used to it, to be honest. I mean, who names their kid Mabel?

Answer? A father who adored his mother.

I respect that. And since my grandmother was a kick-ass woman, I raise my chin and reply, "My grandmother was the coolest person I ever knew. I'm proud of my name."

I said that last night as well.

"Okay then." He turns away from me and continues talking to the person next to him. Luckily, the bartender, a woman almost as old as my grandmother had been when she passed, asks, "What'll you have?"

"I'll, uh, have the 1970 Coochie Cutter, please." The same thing Misty and I had. It's a slushy drink, absolutely yummy, and it only costs three bucks.

"Sure thing, honey."

I'm fiddling around, trying—and failing—to get comfortable on my antiquated barstool, when a deep voice asks, "Is your name really Mabel?"

Why would I make that up? If I were to have a bar name, it'd be something like Shanna or Penelope—*not* Mabel.

Without looking to my left, I sigh. "Yes. It's really Mabel."

The deep voice chuckles. I find that both rude and annoying at the same time. Luckily, Val, the bartender (I know her name is Val because she's wearing a name tag), sets my drink in front of me. I wish I could tell you it's a pretty cocktail with a garnish, but I can't. It's in a red plastic cup with a straw sticking out.

Wrapping my lips around the straw, I suck in the wonderful cool drink.

"I was named after my grandfather on my mother's side."

It's the deep voice again. Still sucking on my straw, I look left and nearly choke at the sight of him.

In a word, he's gorgeous.

Older than me, I suspect, by about ten years. I say that due to the silver flecks in his five o'clock shadow and on his temple. His eyes are silvery blue like a wolf's, and the crinkles around his eyes tell me he's amused. Ignoring that, I continue my assessment. He's got a scar, a small one running through his left eyebrow. No hair grows over the cut. That's okay. We've all got scars. Some inside, some out. What's not okay is his rude question. So, I counter with, "What's your name?"

"Leo."

"Leo?" I snort. "Like the lion?"

"Leonardo. I suppose you could simplify it to lion, but it means 'brave as a lion,' if we're getting technical."

I wasn't.

I can do him one better. "Well, Mabel means lovable."

He gives me a snort of his own.

See what I mean? *Rude.*

"You a Yankee?"

Word to the wise, if you're from "the North" and you visit "the South," plan on getting asked that question. Since I have the thickest Chicago accent there is, it's pretty dang obvious. I'll have to do my best to tone that down while I'm here, though. I know enough about the true Georgians that they don't take to us northerners easily.

"Chicago."

"The Windy City."

"You ever been?"

He chuckles. "Not to Chicago, no. I've heard good things, though."

I shrug. "It's okay."

"What brings you down here, Yank?

"A new job."

"Ah. I see." The man, Leo, sips from his bottle of beer and doesn't say much else. Feeling awkward, I take one more sip of my drink, then slide off my seat. Better not drink any more if I want to drive home. Besides, it's enough that I came here alone; something I'll be doing a lot of now that I've relocated. Might as well get used to it.

"You leavin'?" Leo the lion asks in a fairly thick southern accent. A Savannah accent.

Yes. It's a thing. Grandma Mabel had it. Born and raised in the area, it was distinct.

"Yep." No need to elaborate. I slap a five-dollar bill on the counter.

"Nice to meet ya, Mabel."

"Same, Leo. Same."

chapter three

THIS IS IT. MY FIRST DAY AT THE FORSYTH STREET LIBRARY. I GOT UP extra early to mentally prepare. It might not have been the best idea because rather than preparing, I've had extra time to get even more nervous. So much so my stomach hurts. Not a good start to the day or this new job.

I stare into the full-length mirror that hangs on the back of the door of my grandmother's bedroom and sigh. I haven't had the heart to pack up her things, so her room sits as she left it. I've been using one of the spare bedrooms. I run a hand over the top of my dark brown, nearly black hair. My cut is simple—a chin-length bob with bangs. I've had the same hairstyle since college. I like it because it's easy to maintain and it's good for my round face. Leaning forward, I check my makeup. I've gone light with everything, foundation, pale peachy eye shadow, and mascara to highlight my brown eyes. I skipped my usual red lipstick and black eyeliner for today. Not that anyone will notice the liner since I'll have my tortoiseshell, cat-eye framed glasses on. It's the only part of my attire with any personality.

I chose my most professional outfit, which is a pair of black slacks, a black blazer, and a white polyester blouse. My shoes are black, too, and painful to wear due to the two-inch heel, but they're my only dress shoes. Stepping back, I take a moment to stare at myself. My pants are tight, telling me I've gained weight since the last time I wore them. When was that? At my old job in Chicago.

Glancing down at my lower half, I frown. If my ass gets any wider, I'm going to need to size up. Ordinarily, I'm fine with my curves, but right now, I don't feel my best. My weight has always fluctuated. Whose doesn't? It's when I feel like this, crappy, I know I'm not taking care of myself. My life has been nothing but stress for six months with the loss of my grandmother, my job, my apartment, and my cheating ex. Anyone with all of that drama is bound to add a few pounds. Right?

To be sure, I take a selfie and send it off to Misty in a text asking, "Is this outfit okay?"

I don't have to wait long for her reply. "You look awesome. You're gonna slay at your new job, girrrrrrrl."

Peering into the mirror again, I force a smile on my face, then utter a daily affirmation. "This job is going to be awesome. I'm going to slay. Everyone will love you. You'll make new friends, do all sorts of fun things, and it'll all even out." Reflected in the mirror is a photo that sits on my grandmother's dresser of her when she was in her twenties. Funny, in the photo, her hair is cut in the same style as mine. Her smile seems to be directed at me right now—a sign, perhaps—giving me a little encouragement. Turning, I look at the photo of Grandma Mabel. "Everything will be okay. Right, g'ma?"

As expected, I get no reply. Sighing, I look into the mirror one last time and grumble, "God, I'm nervous."

I MET SEVERAL OF THE BOARD MEMBERS AND THE LIBRARY MANAGER that was leaving during the interview process, but I haven't met any of the other staff. Nor have I ventured into the library since I arrived less than a week ago. I thought that might be a bit, well, weird. Misty and I passed the building on some of our walks, both agreeing that it was one of the most beautiful libraries we'd ever seen.

The building is old, opening in 1916, and the architecture reflects that with its grand staircase that leads up to a neoclassical building. The large front doors are flanked by two enormous columns with Ionic capitals. Capitals are the things at the top of a Greek column. I remember all that thanks to an art history class I took as a graduate student in library science. I know the Ionic columns are seen as feminine with the swirls on either side of the capital. My professor told us an easy way to remember the key points about that style: the curls reminded her of Princess Leia's hair in *Star Wars*. Her example gave me a clear visual, and that stuck with me ever since.

I've been sitting in my vehicle for several minutes when someone knocks on my window. Pressing the button, a woman about my age smiles at me. She's got long strawberry blonde hair that flows in waves down her back. She's wearing a pretty floral dress that she's paired with an ivory-hued cardigan with pearl buttons. Maybe I'm overdressed. I glance down at my black pantsuit and shrug internally. Nothing I can do about that now.

"You the new library manager?"

"I am."

She extends her hand out for me to shake. "I'm Victoria Beauregard." She pronounces her name just like you'd expect a southern belle to speak it—with a little arrogance as it rolls off her tongue. Then the last three letters just sort of float off. It's beautiful, honestly. Maybe I'll adopt that accent since I'm now a Savannahian.

I shake her hand. Her grip is weak; she's barely holding my hand while I know I'm squeezing the bejeezus out of hers.

What? It's the way my dad taught me. "You can tell a lot about a person by the way they shake your hand, Mabel," he said. "A weak handshake is a sign they can't be trusted." I don't know how much of that is true, especially in the South. Women are, well, different here. Genteel is the word I'd use to describe them. Ladylike is another.

Ignoring her limp handshake, I add, "Mabel Frye."

"Nice to meet you, Mabel Frye." She titters. It sounds more like a tinkling than a laugh. "Well, come on in. We're not gonna bite."

I quickly exit my vehicle and decide to lock it since I'll be in the building all day. Maybe longer. Following her up the front steps, I smile at the words carved above the door. "Make Books Thy Comrades." I've already done that. The first time my parents read to me, I was hooked, and nothing has changed in all that time.

Victoria holds the door for me. As I cross the threshold, she says the oddest thing. Odd because it's accompanied by a smirk. "Good luck, Ms. Frye." She steps past me, making her high heels click-clack on the marble floor as I ponder her words.

Shaking off my negative thoughts, I walk up to the information desk. "May I help you?" asks a woman in her seventies. She's got a full head of silver hair that's been teased and hair sprayed into mercy. My grandmother used to go to the "beauty parlor" every two weeks to have her hair done. Then, she'd sleep in rollers and a head scarf. I'd often ask her if it was uncomfortable, but she'd just chuckle saying, "I'm used to it, Mabes."

That's what she used to call me. It's also how she addressed the letter to me in the will. But I don't want to talk about that. It'll make me cry, and the last thing I want to do on the first day of my new job is cry.

"Can I help you?"

"Um, yes." I smile at the older lady. "I'm starting my new job today." I pull my phone out of my purse and search my messages. "I was told to ask for…"

"You're Mabel." She blinks rapidly. "I haven't seen you in years." She's starting to look a little emotional. "I saw the memo announcing the new library manager. I was hoping it was you."

She reaches for a tissue. "My goodness. You're the spittin' image of your grandmother."

"Uh, I..." I have no idea who this woman is.

"Your grandmother and I were thick as thieves." She sniffles. "I'm so sorry for your loss."

"Me too." I nod. Do I know this woman? "What's your name?"

"I'm RuthAnn Clemmons. Your grandmother used to call me Ruthie."

I remember a Ruthie. "Didn't you play cards with Grandma?"

"I did." She giggles. "Your grandmother was quite a card player."

"She cheated." It's my turn to snicker.

"Oh. We were well aware. She never tried the same sneaky tactics twice. It made it fun to figure out what she was up to. It was as much a part of the game as the cards."

My grandma was a stitch, always the life of the party. And extremely clever.

"So, you need to see Mr. Booth, our human resources director."

"Yes. That's right."

"Well, you're going to go down this hallway until you can't go any further and take a sharp right. His office is at the end of that hallway."

"Got it." I nod.

"Have a wonderful day, Mabel. We'll have to have lunch sometime." She winks. "Or happy hour. I know the best place for a *very* dirty martini."

"Sounds perfect." It's not quite nine in the morning, and I'm already on board for a drink. "Yes. Let's do that." I give her a sincere smile. She's made me feel at ease—something I needed badly. "Thanks, Ruthie."

"Good seein' you, Mabel." She beams. "My goodness, I love saying that. Probably said that same thing to your grandma a million times. It's like she's back."

I wish that were true.

RUTHIE'S DIRECTIONS WERE SPOT ON. I FOUND MR. THOMAS BOOTH'S office easily. I knock and have to wait a second. "Come in."

Turning the knob, I push open the door to one of the tiniest offices I've ever seen. There's barely enough room for his desk and a chair probably due to the three tall filing cabinets. Definitely no room for a second chair.

Mr. Booth is a man in his mid-to-late forties, mostly bald but with a smattering of sandy blond hair on either side of his head, and a tiny, dark mustache. He reminds me of John Waters. You know the film director? His mustache is the part about Mr. Booth that gives me pause. It's a tad creepy. Shoot. I shouldn't judge. He's probably a very nice person. Shame on me. I'll ignore his facial hair and get to know him. "Hello." I smile brightly.

He doesn't return the smile. I get a frown instead. "Oh. Maybelle. Let me get your onboarding packet, and we'll move out to one of the conference rooms."

Maybelle? "Sure." I step back out into the hallway. I watch as he gathers materials together.

As he passes, I blurt, "Nice office."

He doesn't laugh. As a matter of fact, I do believe he gives me the stink eye. "It's what happens when the staff had no say or input in the renovations."

The library has undergone extensive renovations over the past two years. I read online that they raised nearly three million dollars from small donations, and then a wealthy benefactor matched that. It enabled them to renovate an entire floor for a children's library that is, from the photos, adorable. They built a life-size doll house for children to wander in and out of, not to mention they've added modern, colorful touches to this old building without diminishing the historic structure. The little I've seen of it is impressive. I hope I'll get a tour before I have to fill out forms.

No such luck.

When I asked Mr. Booth about a tour, he said I needed to complete my paperwork before anything else happens, adding, "I'll see if someone has time to show you around."

Well, damn. I get the sense he doesn't like me. Which is too bad because I'm awesome. I give myself an internal pat on the back because while I'm kidding about being awesome, I do have a positive self-worth and confidence in my abilities. *Thank you, Grandma, Mom, and Dad.*

So, now I'm stuck in a conference room at a large table. Facing a large window, I've noticed people walk by and peek in while pretending not to see me. No doubt trying to get a glimpse of the new boss. I've waved and smiled at each one, but only one or two people gestured back.

I wonder what that's all about.

I suspect there are several things at play. I'm a northerner for one. I remember whenever Grandma introduced me to people around Isle of Hope or Savannah, quite a few frowned after she mentioned I was from up north. Even after a hundred years, people down here are still upset about the North. The other issue most likely relates to my new position. Maybe they all had someone else in mind for the job. I know the drill. I've worked enough places to know how this internal office drama works.

No matter. I'm sure, once they get to know me, they'll love me.

chapter four

THEY HAVEN'T WARMED UP TO ME AND DEFINITELY DON'T LOVE ME.

It's been three and half weeks since I started this sucky job, and everyone is just as standoff-ish as they were before. Maybe worse. I've tried everything in my arsenal to show them how nice and personable I can be by doing things like baking cookies for the staff and inviting everyone out after work for a drink—on me. Only Ruthie showed up. She told me to give it more time. Because I'm the type of person who can't wait around for people to pull their heads out of their backsides, I decided, if they won't come to me *off* the clock, they'll have to do it *on* the clock. I scheduled mandatory one-on-one meetings with each employee and volunteer so I could get to know them. Great idea, right?

It would have been if anyone showed up for their pre-arranged time slot. I had to track every employee down when it came time for their meeting. Like it was choreographed in advance, each one of them gave me a look of shock telling me they'd been *so busy they'd forgotten* and other bullshit excuses like that. Hell, even the human resources guy, Thomas, who insists I refer to him as Mr. Booth, feigned ignorance when his appointment came and went.

In the end, I met with *almost* everyone. I'd prepared a list of several general questions for each person, hoping that it would start a dialogue, like "What's your favorite book?" Perfect, right? I mean, we all work in a library. I also typed up several questions to use if I sensed the person was uncomfortable, my favorite being "If you were any kind of animal, what would it be and why?" I love that question. Or I used to love it. It's one of my top five interview questions. You can learn a lot about a person by a) their reaction to the question. Did they smile? Laugh? Frown? And b) by their response. You know you've got trouble if the person says something like "A mouse" or worse if it's "A tarantula." Still, it's interesting to hear people explain the rationale behind their choice.

First up was Victoria Beauregard, our circulation assistant and the same woman I met in the parking lot on my first day. For our one-on-one, she sat in the chair across from me in the conference room and responded to my questions with a lot of mm-hms and head nods as she tapped her long, pink fingernails on the table in a slow, rhythmic beat. It never wavered. It wasn't a nervous kind of tapping; it was slow and intentional. It put me on edge if I'm being honest. But I forged on. "What's your favorite book?" I asked.

"*Harry Potter*."

"Which one?"

"All of them."

Okay. If you're an avid reader, sure, you might choose *Harry Potter*, but everybody has a favorite. Everybody.

"You don't have a favorite?"

She rolled her eyes. Still tapping her nails, she shrugged. "The first one."

I decided to set her up. "*Harry Potter and the Prisoner of Azkaban*?"

"Sure. That one."

Anyone who's read or even seen the *Harry Potter* series knows *that* is not the first book in the series. It's the third book. After that, I went for the animal question. Her response surprised me.

"A cockroach."

"A cockroach? Why?"

Still tapping, I get another shrug. "They never die. Even in a nuclear explosion."

"Okaaaaay." I can't wait to tell Misty about this. She's gonna laugh until she cries. I'm just going to cry.

In my mind, I shout, "Next!" Except I keep it to myself. I attempted a few other questions without a great deal of luck, so I moved on to the next on my list.

When Pearl Musgrove, our children's librarian, entered the room, she smiled. It gave me high hopes this was going to go better. "What's your favorite book?" I asked.

"Why?"

"Why?" I mean….

"Yes. Why do you need to know that? Is it going in my file?"

"No." I shake my head like I was trying to convince her with just my noggin. "I wanted to get to know you better. We work in a library. I figured…"

"It's none of your business what I do or—" She clears her throat. "—what I read after work."

I could feel the heat rush to my cheeks. Pressing my hand to my face, I attempted to cool myself down to no avail. "Let's move on."

"If you could be…" *Oh, shit.* What's she going to say to this one?

"If I could be what?" She scowls.

"Um. Any kind of animal, what would it be?"

She leans back in her chair and crosses her arms. "What is this? Some kind of psychological examination?"

"No." My head shakes twice as hard and fast as before. "It's a fun question."

"Fun?"

"Yeah." I clear my throat. "I'm just trying to get to know you better."

"Maybe this isn't your forte."

"Asking you questions?"

She shakes her head. "No. Talking." Then, she mumbles, "And managing," but I hear her. That one stung.

In the end, I survived my one-on-ones with every employee and volunteer except one. The person I couldn't nail down was Mr. Thomas Booth. Apparently, he was too busy to meet with me.

Those little one-on-ones were two weeks ago. I'm starting to think time isn't the answer, and that maybe I'm going to have to either accept the fact that these people hate my guts or turn into the kind of boss I detest, a mean one. I'm a great supervisor—all about positive reinforcement and encouragement. I discovered that style of leadership after working for a person who insulted everyone for everything. We're talking playground kind of insults. Because of her, I swore if I ever led people, I'd never be like that, and I've stood by that promise. Until now. Because not only are they acting like I've got the plague but none of them are doing a damn thing I've asked of them either. Well, Ruthie is, but she's a volunteer, and there's only so much she can do around this stupid place.

God. I'm frustrated. A feeling I leave the library with each and every evening. It's why I stop at Parker's convenience store almost every night. Parker's has bottles of Pinot Grigio *and* makes the most amazing fried chicken and mac and cheese. It's to die for. On top of that, they sell home decor. Last Tuesday, I bought the cutest set of oven mitts. They were covered in colorful sprinkle donuts. It's funny, though. My oven no longer works, but when or if it ever starts up again, I'll be ready.

chapter five

"WHAT CAN I GET YA?"

I'm standing at the counter ready to order my usual. Hell, I wonder if I said that to the clerk whose name tag reads Angela, she'd remember. Because it's been just her and me for the last week since I never seem to leave the library until closing. I lose my nerve and repeat my order. "I'll have the Fill-up Box with chicken tenders."

"Side?"

She's asking what I want as my side. "Mac and cheese." Duh.

"Sorry, we're out."

"Ou-out?" I sputter. "But…" I can't believe I'm going to do this, but I've got to plead my case. "But Angela. I've had the worst day ever. I *need* mac and cheese."

That gets a chuckle out of her. "Worst day ever?"

"Yeah." She looks like she's about to give in. I'm thinking maybe Angela has a hidden stash of fresh ooey gooey buttery mac and cheese somewhere in the back. She's sort of smiling at me. Like she *gets* me.

"Your day can't be worse than mine, girl."

"Oh?" I beg to differ. I mean, for starters, the library custodian, Halbert, found something I will never unsee or unsmell in the men's restroom and proceeded to show every staff member and visitor who came in the door. Just thinking about it sort of makes me lose my appetite, but then I realize that has obviously passed. The ringing of the bell over the store entrance, indicating another person coming or going, draws me out of my reminiscence and puts my attention back on the conversation with Angela. "Did you have a bad day too?"

"My kid punched another kid at school, knocking out the other kid's front teeth and bloodying his nose. My kid got suspended, so I'll have to find someone to watch the little convict while I work. And on top of that, the parents are gonna sue." She mutters something like "blood from a turnip" or something along those lines.

"That is pretty bad. How old is your son?"

"Six."

Holy crap.

She sighs. "So, what'll it be?"

"Get the okra. It's pretty good."

Okra? *Pretty* good? Is this person serious? I don't want something that's merely "pretty good." I want the thing that dreams are made of. I turn my head and come face to chest with a plaid flannel shirt. Looking up, I see someone I've seen before but can't quite place him. "Okra is gross."

"Nah. You Yanks don't know what you're missin'."

"We've got potato logs," Angela interjects.

"Those aren't bad. Get those, Mabel."

How does he…? Oh. Wait one second. Pointing rudely at his face, I shake my finger. "You're the guy from Pinkie's."

He holds out his hand like he wants to shake mine. I do it. I place my hand in his, but instead of shaking, he pulls it up and kisses the top of it. "I'm Leo. Leo Watts."

"Right. The lion."

"Roar." He says it softly which makes me laugh. And because I like how his hand feels way too much, I pull it out of his and shove it into the pocket of my black slacks. "How you doin', Yank?"

"Great."

"Didn't sound great." He nods at Angela. "You neither. You want me to talk to those other parents for you?"

They know each other.

"Thanks, Leo. That'd be great. And while you're at it, can you put the fear of God into Clarence?"

"I'll give it a try." He chuckles. "Something tells me I'm gonna be doing a lot of that in the future."

"Bite that tongue of yours, Leo." She laughs. "Got your order right here." I watch as Angela steps around the counter with two containers. I recognize those boxes. One contains fried chicken, and the other huge, round one is filled—no, it's *heaping*—with macaroni and cheese. So much so, I can see the poor little macaroni noodles squished against the lid that barely fits. "Hey," I say, putting my hands on my hips. "You took all of the cheesy noodle goodness."

He shrugs. "I called in my order ahead of time. They always run out."

"B-but…"

"But, what?" He stares down at me, waiting, it seems.

"But I *need* that." I point at his food.

"Nobody *needs* this, Yank." He holds up the container. I swear to you, I can see the steam rising from the top of it. It smells divine. "All we need is air, water, and—"

"That." I point again. "My day sucked donkey balls, Leo. A day like that calls for comfort food, and there's nothing more comforting than that."

He chuckles. I'm not sure if he's laughing *at* me or what.

"Donkey balls?"

"Yeah. Donkey balls."

"I've never heard that turn of a phrase before. You're quite a wordsmith."

"So I've been told." I nod at his food. "Well? Are you gonna share?"

"Share?" He looks over at Angela. "Should I share with the Yank?"

"She's all right, Leo." She shrugs. "Maybe a small dish?" She looks at me.

"Yes. That'd be great." I nod. "If you'd be so kind, Leo." I flutter my lashes at him and give him my best puppy dog eyes. "Pretty please."

He shakes his head. "Never do that again."

"What?"

"Beg."

I'm taken aback. "I was just kidding." The nerve of this guy.

He hands Angel the container. "Give her half."

"No." I start to turn and wave it off. "Never mind." The dick-faced ass-face. I'm so angry right now. Fed up, honestly. With my job, my life, and especially this rude, rude man. Even if he is gorgeous, it doesn't excuse him saying something like that. I can beg if I effing want to.

"Ah, come now, honey. I want to share."

"No." *The jerk.* I'm out the door and at my car before I realize I just walked out with a bottle of wine. A bottle I didn't pay for. "Crap."

Stepping back into the store, it seems as though no one noticed. Thank goodness. The last thing I need is the police getting involved and adding to this shitstorm of a Monday.

Yeah. It's *only* Monday.

I rush to the cashier, set the bottle on the counter, and race back out to my car because heading my way is Leo. The ill-mannered guy wearing hot flannel *in May* in Savannah, Georgia. Dumb. It's hot already.

Getting behind the wheel, I throw my purse into the passenger seat, start my car, and gun it (as much as you can an old hybrid) out of the parking lot. The second I reach the stop sign a block away, I want to scream. I walked away without any food. No chicken. No mac and cheese. Hell, I didn't even bother getting the wine.

I've got two choices. I can either go home and eat the old can of chicken noodle soup in my cupboard, or I can turn around and get what I deserve.

"HE'S NOT SO BAD, LADY." ANGELA'S DEFENDING LEO. "HE'S EASY on the eyes too." She winks at me. "Single, last I heard."

"Good for him," I grumble. Except when I make that snide little remark, part of me is glad to hear it.

No, Mabel. Adding a man into your craptastic life isn't the way to go.

"He told me to hang on to the mac and cheese in case you came back."

"He did?" Well, that was nice of him. I guess. *No. I'm not going to forgive or excuse him.* Although, he didn't do anything truly terrible. Telling me not to "beg" isn't that bad, but it just stung because I thought I was being adorable. Guess not.

"He did." I watch her add chicken strips into the box, making sure she gives me three good ones. There's nothing worse than opening a box up to find three spindly little chicken strips. Am I right?

"Dipping sauce?"

"Ranch, please." I don't actually dip my chicken in anything. I save those packets in the off chance I make a salad at home or cut up some celery.

I snort at those thoughts.

Like I'm going to eat vegetables. Especially celery. Ick.

With food in hand, I bypass the wine. I've been drinking way too much. They say it takes six weeks to develop a habit, and I'm on week four. If I stop now, I'll be in good shape. Maybe if I only drink every *other* night…

The other habit I need to break is stopping at Parker's altogether. My black pants are getting tighter, and my bank account is shrinking little by little. I need to save so I can keep the house standing. Literally.

Sighing, I shoot off a text to my bestie. "I've had the day from hell. Let's talk tonight." Even though she doesn't respond right away, I know I'll hear from her at some point in the evening. I can always count on Misty.

I get back into my car and head east out of Savannah to Isle of Hope. To the house I love but don't think I can keep because I don't have the time, skills, or honestly, the money to fix it like it deserves.

chapter six

Taking the first step up onto my porch, I hear the telltale sign of wood cracking. I also feel some give under my feet. I knew the steps leading up to the house were touch and go, but I'd hoped they'd last longer than a month. The good news? I know how to use a hammer and nails. I also know if I go to the store that sells wood, that someone there will cut a piece the size I need. I've done it before, you know, *begged*. Fluttering my eyelashes is nearly one hundred percent effective. Before tonight it was, anyway. That man, Leo, ruined my streak.

I'm not going to think about him or the step. I'm going to grab a glass of water, then come back out and sit on my porch and eat my dinner. The temperature has cooled quite a bit, and there's a subtle breeze coming in from the east. I can smell the ocean from my spot on the porch, and that soothes my nerves a lot. My sign is Aquarius, born February 9th. My grandma used to tell me that meant I was happiest near water. I'm not sure that's true, but I know the few times we went to the beach here were some of the happiest days of my life.

Maybe Grandma was right.

With water and a fork in hand, I plop down and salivate thinking about my food. The first bite of mac and cheese causes me to close my eyes and moan. It's that good. Even a little cold, it's so frigging delicious. My mind is on food when I feel something rub against my leg. I know who, or what, that is. It's a cat. He's been here almost every night—at least the nights I've come out onto my porch. He must've smelled the food. He's—at least I think—a male. Either way, he loves Parker's chicken as much as I do.

"You want some chicken?" I bend to scratch the top of his head. He's a yellow tabby. I suppose he could be more tiger than tabby, but I'm no feline expert. I should grab a book on different breeds in the library.

I groan. "The library was horrible today, Dewey."

Yes. I named him. It's hard to talk to someone if you don't know their name. Since he doesn't wear a collar, I had to come up with something on my own, and Dewey, of the Dewey Decimal System, seemed apropos.

Tossing a hunk of chicken in front of him, he purrs loudly as he eats. "You hungry, big guy?" He is a big cat. Tall, if there's such a thing. "So, let me tell you about my day."

What?

He's what we call a captive audience. He'll hang around until the chicken's gone. I've got some time.

"The staff still hates me. Except Ruthie. She said she's been investigating the reason why everyone acts like I've got the plague, but so far, all she can tell is it appears to be an organized attempt to get me to quit."

Ha. I can't quit. I'm stuck here. "Which stinks, Dewey, because…" I feel myself tear up. I don't like to cry, but because it's just me and Dewey, I'll let it slide. "…I'm a nice person. I really am. I'm… I'm fun." Oh, crud. The tears are really coming now. I've been holding them in for weeks trying to be strong like I suspect my grandmother would have wanted. Hell, she used to say, "Never let 'em see you cry, Mabes. Wait until you get home."

"She was a wise woman, Dewey." I sniffle, then use the napkin that came with my dinner to blow my nose. "Anyway, besides the deal with Halbert, I discovered that someone has been reshelving the books wrong." It wasn't just one book. It was at first. When I reshelved the first book in the right place, I found another book that was wrong. That went on for two straight hours. I had asked our archivist, Sammy, to help. I could tell she didn't want to do it. I know this because she walked around as slow as a sea turtle and sighed each time she found a book out of place. She also looked over her shoulder toward the circulation desk about a thousand times where Victoria stood, glaring back at her.

"From that, I gathered two things, Dewey." One, for some reason, Victoria could be the one behind this orchestrated effort against me, and the other, I needed to find the weakest link to find out why. "I think that weak link might be Sammy." She's young. Too young to be an archivist, which usually requires a bachelor's degree in history or library science, but she explained that she was able to earn her associate degree while still in high school by taking online courses and that the job description didn't specify which type of degree was needed. "I used the time together to chat her up." As they say in jolly ol' England. "I had her laughing at one point this afternoon, which only happened after we moved to the fiction section, out of Victoria's line of sight at the circulation desk. After that, she warmed up to me." I take the last bite of my side dish. "I should take her a gift for helping me." Butter her up some.

Yes. I know it's her job to help where she's needed, but really, she's responsible for the preservation of our historical documents and first editions, not shelving. "I could take her a cookie or something as a thank you." I nod and smile at Dewey who's also finishing up his final piece of chicken. "We're going to need to start eating healthier, Dewey." He meows like he's in pain. "I know. But my pants are all getting tight, and wearing sweatpants to the library is a no-no."

"Good morning, Ruthie." I smile wide at my one and only friend here in Savannah.

"It's gonna be a scorcher today." She likes to start my morning off with a weather report. "This heat is gonna be the death of me."

"I know. May in Chicago is quite cool." Not like here. "At least we're inside most of the day in the air-conditioning." Which is no joke since my old house has no AC and no functioning window air conditioners. I need to splurge on one of those, or I'll be like Ruthie and the heat. Changing the subject, I ask, "Anything I need to know this morning?"

"Victoria called out for today."

I shouldn't smile, but I can't help it. I quickly frown. "Oh. I hope she's okay." That's not completely truthful.

"She said she had the 'sniffles.'"

"She used the word sniffles?"

"She did." Ruthie smirks. "I haven't had the sniffles since I was a young'un."

"Same." No matter. My perceived enemy is going to be gone for the day. Maybe I'll make some headway with the rest of the staff—at the very least Sammy. "All right. I need to work in my office a little bit this morning if anyone is looking for me." Which no one has yet, but what kind of manager would I be if I didn't inform my staff of my whereabouts.

"You betcha, honey."

I take the first set of steps up to the second floor. It's what I'd call a grand staircase made of marble. The steps are wide to accommodate a crowd, something we'll never have to worry about, but it's still one of my favorite features about the library. The entire place has an elegant quality probably due to the materials used to build the original structure. No expense was spared back in 1916. The good old days.

On the second floor, I round the banisters until I reach the staircase that leads to the third floor. This is the level that houses the children's section and my office. I see Pearl at the counter and wave. I get nothing in return. Not a wave or a smile. I don't know why it bothers me so much. It's possible to do my job without everyone liking me. I mean, look at politicians. Maybe that isn't the best example. But you get my drift.

Opening my office door, I step inside. Ordinarily, I make it a rule to keep my door open, the open-door policy and all that, but this morning, shutting it feels right. I boot up my computer and kick off my sneakers. Opening my bottom drawer, I pull out the pair of black heels I wear every day in my attempt to look professional. I check my floral blouse. Well, not mine. It was my grandmother's, and by the colors and the pattern, I'd say it was from the 1970s. I remember her wearing it to church sometimes, and I've always loved it. She has several things that I plan to wear. She had a big personality and with that came bold clothing.

As I was getting dressed this morning, I picked up my boring white blouse and had an epiphany. I asked myself, "Who am I trying to impress at this point?" I was trying to appear subdued and professional in my white blouses and black suit, but at that moment this morning, I decided—no more. I'm going to wear things that make me feel good, confident. *Screw these people.* Today is the first day of the rest of my life and all that shit.

Feeling eyes on me, I peer out my one and only office window and see Pearl looking back. She quickly turns away.

That's another thing I'm changing. As of today, all these people can suck it. I know for a fact the board of directors supports me. So far, they've liked all of my ideas to engage the community. For example, showing a classic film in our new auditorium, free to the public. I also suggested a children's story time, something I was shocked to hear they hadn't adopted yet, but after meeting Pearl, I get why. I've got plans for arts and crafts activities for the young and old, as well as an introduction to creative writing class that I'll teach myself. We desperately need an after school program for kids. One of the best ones we started in Chicago was a Lego club. That drew the kids in, boys and girls, like flies. We created competitive tasks with prizes and had people from the community judge the final projects. It was one of my favorite activities.

One other idea I had was eliminating late fees for overdue books. The board is pondering that notion, but it doesn't seem like that's going to fly. I even backed up my idea with evidence. People with overdue fines don't return to the library even if it's less than one dollar in fines. It would create a bit more work for us to encourage patrons to return books, but I know for a fact Victoria has time on her hands. She can make calls.

Opening my email, I see a message from the chairwoman of the board, Margaret Atkinson, with the subject of "Book Fines."

"Here we go."

I read:

Mabel,

After a long discussion with the board, we would like to give you the opportunity to prove your hypothesis regarding overdue fines. You have six months. Please document all of your data so that we can review that at the end of the time allotted.

Thank you,

M. Atkinson

I can't believe it. I'm so giddy, I clap. Pearl must hear me because she looks my way again, but it's only momentarily.

I feel like celebrating, but it'd be just me. Unless... I pick up my phone and hit Sammy's extension. She answers, "Archives. This is Sammy."

She knows who's calling. We've got caller ID. No matter. "Sammy. I have great news, and I wanted to share it with someone."

There's a pause. "And... you chose me?"

"Yes."

"Why?"

"Because…" Why? "I had fun working with you yesterday, and you were the first person I thought of."

"Oh." Another pause. "All right. What's the good news?"

I explain my idea about overdue fines. "I think that's a good idea, really. It's not like we bring in a ton of revenue off fines."

"Oh, I guess I can see that."

We're a nonprofit organization. The money isn't the point. "I've always felt that penalizing patrons, fellow book lovers, was the wrong way about it. I'm all about positive reinforcement. Let's encourage them to bring the book back by giving them options for their next book. I mean, let's say we're trying to get one of our classics back, *Pride and Prejudice*. We could call them up and say something like 'Hello, Mrs. Featherbottom, if you bring back that book, you could pick up *Persuasion*, another excellent Jane Austen book.'"

I hear Sammy giggle. "Mrs. Featherbottom?"

I laugh too. "Sure. Why not?"

"And was that your attempt at an English accent?" She snickers.

"Not good?"

"No." She pauses. "It was awful."

I gasp. "I beg your pardon, *Guvna*. I've spent a great deal of time watching British television just to hone my accent."

"Um…"

I crack up. "Just kidding."

"Okay. Good. Because it could use some work."

"Noted." I don't want to keep her on the phone too long. I think I'm better off having short interactions with her in order to build her trust in me. It sounds like manipulation on my part, and maybe it is, but I've got to try something. "Well, better get back to it. Thanks for letting me share that news with you, Sammy."

"No problem." And the line goes dead.

"Baby steps, Mabel," I mutter to myself. When I feel eyes on me again, I turn to see Pearl glaring at me.

Shrugging, I mouth, "What?"

She shakes her head and looks away.

Ugh. I kind of wish Pearl would disappear. But that's a terrible thing to think. Right?

chapter seven

"Thanks for coming." It's not like they had a choice in the matter. I look around the conference room at the staff and volunteers of the library. I called a staff meeting, one that will be held the third Thursday of each month from eight to nine in the morning. The library opens at 9:30 a.m. during the week, meaning there's no reason for anyone to miss the meeting. And since I'd made it mandatory, I expect everyone to be here. And almost everyone is. "Has anyone seen Mr. Booth?"

Ruthie is the only one to respond. "I saw him come in at around eight this morning and head in the direction of his office."

"Right." I set my notebook down onto the table next to Ruthie. "Be right back."

I've had about all I can take of Mr. Thomas Booth's bad attitude and avoidance. He's been a real stinker since I started, never answering his phone when I call to ask him important questions. His email responses are autogenerated and say, "Thank you for your correspondence. I will reply at my earliest convenience." Turns out, it's never been convenient for the jerk-face to write me back.

His door is shut, as usual. I knock three times and wait. When there's no response, I lean in and press my ear to the door. Nothing. Knocking again, I pause before turning his doorknob, but when I do, it won't budge. Locked.

"Where are you, Mr. Thomas Booth?"

Giving up, I stomp back to the conference room and see several people have left. "Where did they go?" I ask no one in particular.

Sammy is the one to answer. "Bathroom, I believe."

"Fine." I sigh with irritation. "We'll wait."

I move back to my spot in front of the room. I've got a slide deck ready that's going to cover some of my new plans for the library, including waiving overdue fines. It'll be interesting to see if anyone opposes that plan. It doesn't matter if they do; the board gave it the green light, and that's all that matters. Their job is to execute the plan. That's it.

Minutes pass and I'm about to give up when Pearl strolls back into the room, taking her seat next to Halbert. "Has anyone seen Victoria?"

"She's got an upset stomach." It's Pearl who gives that personal update.

"Oh. Should I check on her?"

Like it was planned, everyone in the room says, "No."

"Fine." Sighing, I realize nearly twenty minutes have passed since the start of this stupid meeting. "Let's give her a few more minutes. If you all need to get a coffee refill, let's break for five and reconvene"—I glance at my watch—"at 8:30."

I've never seen people leave a room so fast. Everyone except Ruthie. "You okay?" she asks softly.

No. I don't tell her that, though. "Sure." I shrug. "Things are slowly getting better. I just need—" My words are halted by a sound I'll never unhear. A bloodcurdling scream. "What the hell?"

Ruthie interjects, "Good heavens!"

Leaving everything behind, I race out the door. Not sure where the scream came from, I look right, then left where Sammy is standing, looking pale. She raises her hand slowly and points toward the fiction stacks. Without a word, I run in the direction she's pointing. A small group of people have gathered at the end of one of the aisles. Moving closer, I notice their heads are all looking down. "What is it?"

The group of six or seven staff and volunteers slowly move back, giving me an opening and a perfect view of the scene before me. "Oh, my God." I can't move, and I can't think of anything else to say when the sound of sobbing breaks me out of my spell.

Someone behind me whispers, "It's-it's Thomas."

They're right about that. On the floor is Mr. Thomas Booth. He's dead. I know that without even taking a pulse.

"What happened?" someone asks.

"Who would have done that?" asks another.

"Should we help him up?" I'm not sure who says that, but I want to giggle at the ridiculous question, though that would be inappropriate. Instead, I shake off my shock and do what a good leader would do. I jump into action. "Ruthie, please call 9-1-1."

"Sure thing, Mabel."

Turning to the group, I attempt a reassuring smile. "Halbert, could you go wait by the front door to let the police in?"

"Sure thing, boss."

"Sammy, would you please place a sign on the door telling our patrons that we are closed for the day due to..." Due to what?

"Water line break." I'm not sure who suggests that, but it's a good excuse. "Perfect. A water line break."

"Okay, Mabel." Sammy turns and moves in the direction of the circulation desk. She looks visibly shaken.

Maybe I should've chosen someone else, then again, perhaps keeping her busy will be good? Shit. I don't know. I'm faking all this leadership crap. Still, I keep it up. "Everyone else, please go back to the conference room and wait for the police. I'm sure they're going to need to question each of us."

"Why?" squeaks Marlene, one of our front desk volunteers. "I didn't do *that*." She gestures wildly at the dead man.

"It's just procedure." I attempt to reassure her even if I have no idea what's going to happen since the only murders I've ever encountered have been in books. When everyone scatters, I turn back to the scene before me. He's dead, for sure. There's so much blood, he can't have any left inside. He's lying prone. His face is turned enough that I can see his eyes are open. At least his left eye is open. His left arm is next to his body, but his right arm is up—his hand resting on the ground above his head. It's not empty; he's clutching something. And that something is a book.

I scan the aisle again and see the books on the shelf to my left are a jumbled mess with about twenty to thirty books on the floor leading to and around the body. There's also a trail of blood starting at the other end of the aisle to his spot on the floor, like he tried to walk after he was stabbed in the back. Bending to get a closer look at the item in his back, it's obvious it's a large pair of silver scissors. They're actually sewing scissors. And the reason I know this? Because they're mine. Well, they were my grandmother's sewing shears. They're mine now.

"Fuck," I mutter. Whoever killed Mr. Thomas Booth used *my* scissors. "That's just great." Shaking off the irritation of knowing I'll be the number one suspect, I pull my phone out of my pocket and take a few photos of the scene. I'm not sure why; it's just a gut feeling I have that I'm going to need those. Squatting down, I'm so tempted to pull the book out of his hand. Something about this scene before me makes me feel as though the book is significant. I could be wrong. He was probably just clutching at anything to hang on, trying to get to safety, to get help.

Poor Mr. Thomas Booth.

I'm broken from my thoughts when I hear footsteps, a bunch of them, clomping up the marble steps. Then, voices. Well, one in particular. "I'm Detective Watts. Where's the body?"

I'm not sure who he's speaking to, but I step back and see a man I've seen one too many times. Leo Watts.

When he looks up, I almost feel a smile cross my lips, but then I remember why he's here. I point at Mr. Booth. "He's here."

Leo stomps over, his face fierce. "You haven't touched anything, have you?"

Like I'm a novice. Any reader of mystery or suspense knows you don't touch anything at a crime scene, or you'll be suspect numéro uno. Glancing at my scissors, I frown. "No. Of course not. I cleared the area, asking my staff to stay in the conference room to wait for...." I pause. "You, I guess."

"Fine." He sighs and runs a hand through his hair. "You can run along. Go wait with the others."

"But..."

"Let me do my job, Miss..." His brow furrows. "It's miss right?"

I don't bother with all of that. "I'm just Mabel Frye."

"Let us do our job, Mabel Frye."

"But..." He's turned away before I've gotten a chance to finish my statement. I watch as Leo moves over to a group of three other cops. There are two in Savannah police department uniforms, and another, like Leo, in a suit. Before I'm forcibly removed, I want to check out one more thing. Squatting, I'm able to contort myself enough to see the spine of the book. It's not necessary for me to read the entire title. The first two words above his bloodied fingers are enough. "To Kill..." I frown. "*To Kill a Mockingbird*?"

Now *that's* interesting.

sneak peek

Mabel Frye:Accidental Private Eye–
Murder in the Stacks

chapter 1

"What's going to happen now? Will we have to stay in this room all day?" Martin, our high school summer intern asks nervously.

We've been sequestered in the one of the conference rooms in the Forsyth Public Library until the police finish their investigative work in the fiction stacks. That's where we discovered the body of Mr. Thomas Booth, the library's human resources director. He'd been stabbed in the back with a large pair of scissors.

I scan the room again making sure everyone is accounted for.

When my eyes land on Pearl Musgrove, children's librarian, I'm surprised to see how red and blotchy her face is—like she's been crying. When our eyes meet, she looks expectant, like she's waiting for me to answer Martin's question. Because I'm supposed to be their leader, I respond based on no real information only from things I remember from books and television shows, "I believe they'll need to question everyone before we can leave."

I stand to peer out the conference room window and see nothing but our second-floor circulation desk. This conference room has one wall of windows that faces.... I have to think for a moment... south. From this room, we can see a portion of our non-fiction section. The murder happened in fiction, which is out this door, around the corner, and technically behind this room if you consider the wall of windows the front.

Leaning out, I look to my left for any activity, but I can't see a dang thing. I return to my seat and sigh. I'm getting tired of sitting here too. Taking my phone from my suit jacket pocket, I note the time. "It's nearly noon." I say to no one in particular. Ten of us, consisting of employees and library volunteers, have been sitting in this room for two and a half hours. I called a staff meeting for 8:30 this morning. We discovered his body close to nine after which, we called the police and have been here ever since. Honestly, it's kind of ridiculous. What's taking so dang long?

Victoria Beauregard, our circulations librarian, looks pale, sickly. With a shaking voice, she asks, "Who would want to kill Tommy?"

Tommy? That's interesting since he insisted I call him Mr. Booth.

I wait as Victoria says more. "He couldn't hurt a fly. He loved animals."

I want to laugh at Victoria's words. Does she think flies are animals? I keep it to myself because she's full-on crying now. Then, she asks, "What about Boudreaux?"

"Boudreaux?" I can't help wanting to know more.

She frowns at my question but explains, "His poor, little doggy." Victoria is full-on bawling now.

Pearl slides over to the chair next to her and wraps an arm over her shoulder. "Shh, darlin'. It's going to be okay. We'll drive over to his house after this and check on him."

I had no idea Pearl and Victoria were so tight. I've never seen them speak to each other except to say "hello" and "goodbye". Plus, if you're going by age and appearance alone, they're polar opposites. Not that it matters. Opposites attract.

The fact that they're close and they know where Mr. Booth lives, well, lived, is interesting. Maybe all of these people are friends. Perhaps they hang out at each other's places on Saturday nights having mint juleps or something. Lord knows they wouldn't invite me to their little shindigs.

I feel my face heat with irritation. Almost anger. Why, suddenly, do I feel angry with these people? I knew where I stood with them from the very beginning. There was no pretense. No false sense of solidarity. The only person who gives me the time of day is Ruthie and sometimes Sammy.

Shake if off, Mabel.

With Victoria sobbing into Pearls cardigan sweater, the one she wears every single day, I ask, "What was he like outside of work?"

My question was met with silence. "I mean. Did he have other hobbies? Friends? Did he like to have any fun?"

"How dare you?" Surprisingly, that question comes from Halbert, our custodian.

I turn to look him square in the eye and I'm taken aback by how angry he is. "It's none of your damn business what he was like outside of work, lady."

Lady?

I had hopes Halbert was warming up to me, but I guess not. Not one to let things go, I ask. "Excuse me?"

"You know what?" he snaps. "I think *you* killed him."

"Me?" I squeak. Several people mutter their agreement as heads nod. "Why would *I* kill Mr. Booth? I barely knew the man." Duh. I was *just* asking what he was really like.

"Because he's the one that told us all to treat you like a—like a…"

Halbert can't seem to come up with the next word. Pearl can. "Leper."

"He did?" That's news to me. "Why?" I'm sincerely curious. What in the hell did I ever do to Mr. Thomas Booth?

I could stop calling him by his entire name but after a month and a half, it's now a habit.

Everyone, please…." Ruthie sighs. "It doesn't do a damn bit of good to point fingers. Let the police do their jobs. The sooner they do, the sooner we can leave."

"How long do you think the library will be closed?" Sammy, thankfully, changes the subject. She doesn't look any better than Victoria. She's pale and shaky. "A week? A month?" She bites her lip. "I can't go without a job. I need the money."

It's a question I hadn't considered. "I'm not sure. It'll depend on how long the police will need access to the library and on the board of directors." Which reminds me. I'd better give Margaret Atkinson, the chairman of the library board, a call. "Excuse me."

"Where do you think *you're* going?" Pearl asks sounding every bit as resentful as she does every other day except there's a tone that I hadn't heard before, commanding. Like she believes she's in charge now.

She's not.

Still, I'll give her the benefit of the doubt and answer as respectfully as I can muster, "I'm going to my office to grab Mrs. Atkinson's number."

I step out of the conference room and run right into a dark suit, possibly navy but closer to black and a blue dress shirt covered broad chest. "Miss Frye?"

I look up at the face of a man I've seen a lot lately, Leo Watts.

Detective Leo Watts. Except the few times we've met, I didn't know he was a cop. "Yes?"

"Where do you think you're going?"

"To my office. I need to grab a phone number."

"No."

I blink. "No?" He can't tell me what I can and can't do. Wait. Yes, he can. Still, it doesn't hurt to ask, "Why not?"

"Everybody in that room is a suspect."

I assumed that. We were the only people here at the time of the murder.

"Which means, every square inch of this place needs to be examined. That includes offices, telephones, and personal belongings."

"I need to call Margaret Atkinson to tell her what's going on."

"I'll give Maggy a call." He stares down into my eyes.

His are gray blue with dark lashes that are longer than they have a right to be. "Maggy?" *He knows Margaret?*

"We go way back. She was my high school English teacher."

"Ah." I didn't know she'd been a teacher.

"She retired from teaching and now volunteers. Does a lot of stuff for the community." He leans a tad closer. So much so, I can smell him. It's a nice smell. Kind of musky. Just giving the scent a name has my mind wondering if it's his soap or his cologne. If it's soap, does he rub it all over his big, muscular body or…?

Stop, Mabel. Now is not the time to let your mind wander straight down into the gutter. A man is dead in the fiction stacks, for cripes sake. Have some decorum.

I blink realizing Leo's still talking. "…old money. Her family is pretty important around these parts."

These parts? He sounds like he's from an old western movie.

"You'll call her?"

"I will." He nods at the door to the conference room. "Now. Get on back in there. We'll be with you all shortly."

It wasn't shortly. It was another hour before they started questioning us. It's a good thing, too, because the people in the room, my staff, were starting to go all *Lord of the Flies* on me. In the over three or so hours we were waiting, I watched as the staff attempted to overthrow my leadership and install Pearl into my job since I was "probably the killer".

Ruthie and I, with a little help from Sammy, were able to persuade everyone to remain calm and convince some of those volunteers and employees on the fence about my guilt or innocence, I had no reason to kill Mr. Booth. But what was interesting about that assumption is it turns out the reason Mr. Thomas Booth despised me is due to the fact he'd applied for my job as manager of the Forsyth Public Library but was passed over for me. I suspect it's also why he avoided me like the plague.

Pre-order your copy of *Mabel Frye: Accidental Private Eye, Murder in the Stacks* on Amazon.com.

about the author

Kayt grew up in the midwest surrounded by a loving family, which included three brothers, one sister, and parents who always fostered her creative side.

She wrote her first book when she couldn't find a story about a certain type of a woman and a specific kind of man. She called it "Game Changer," and in couldn't have been a more appropriate title. It changed her life in many ways.

Her author goal is to write stories that romance readers can relate to, while making readers laugh and sometime shed a tear or two. Kayt hopes her readers can escape into a fantasy, one that's actually possible.

Sure, some of the stories are dubbed "insta-love," but that's okay. She fell in love with her husband pretty damn fast and with her daughter the second she saw her.

facebook.com/authorkaytmiller

twitter.com/kaytmiller1

instagram.com/kaytmiller1

bookbub.com/profile/kayt-miller

acknowledgments

Thank you to Hot Tree Editing for editing this book from start to finish.

And an extra special thank you to Becky at Hot Tree Promotions for your advice, expertise, and her positivity.

Thanks to Heather for listening to my ideas and reading this as I went along!

Thanks to my Hopeful Romantic Beta readers! *(You know who you are.)* You're the best!

also by kayt miller

For more information:
www.kaytmiller.com

series: mabel frye: accidental private eye

stand-alones

The Virginia Chronicles

series: pick-up lines

Cranky Pants: Pick-up Lines Book 1

Lucky Charmer: Pick-up Lines Book 2

Double Dog Dare: Pick-up Lines Book 3

series: bedhead

Bedhead (Book 1)

Redhead (Book 2)

Deadhead (Book 3)

Wedhead (Book 4)

series: the flynns

Out of the Blue: The Flynns Book One

Mick'sology: The Flynns Book Two

Vested Interest: The Flynns Book Three

The Importance of Being Ernie: The Flynns Book Four

The Importance of Being Kennedy's: The Flynns Book Five

Quirky Girl: The Flynns Book Six

The Art of the Game

series: the palmer sisters

Lainie: The Palmer Sisters Book 1

Agatha: The Palmer Sisters Book 2

Sadie: The Palmer Sisters Book 3

Cortland: The Palmer Sisters Book 4

box sets: the palmer sisters